RECRUITED

Suzanne Weyn

D0062451

SURVIVING SOUTHSIDE

RECRUITED

Suzanne Weyn

darbycreek

MINNEAPOLIS

Darby Creek
A division of Lerner Publishing Group, Inc.
241 First Avenue North
Minneapolis, MN 55401 U.S.A.

Website address: www.lernerbooks.com

The images in this book are used with the permission of:
© Image Source/Getty Images, (main image) front cover;
© iStockphoto.com/Jill Fromer, (banner background) front cover
and throughout interior; © iStockphoto.com/Naphtalina, (brick
wall background) front cover and throughout interior.

Library of Congress Cataloging-in-Publication Data

Weyn, Suzanne.
        Recruited / Suzanne Weyn.
            p.   cm. — (Surviving Southside)
        ISBN: 978–0–7613–6153–4 (lib. bdg. : alk. paper)
        [1. Football—Fiction. 2. High schools—Fiction.
    3. Schools—Fiction. 4. African Americans—Fiction.]
    I. Title
    PZ7.W539Rd 2011
    [Fic]—dc22   2010023662

Manufactured in the United States of America
1 – BP – 12/31/10

For Robert, Brendan,
and Emmett Maloney,
with love.
—S.W.

CHAPTER 1

K adeem Jones tried not to stare at the far corner of the football field. A bunch of middle-aged men had gathered there.

The men were dressed casually. They wore baseball caps, sporty jackets, and jeans. They spoke to one another casually, joking and laughing. But their eyes were on the football players the whole time.

Kadeem needed to forget they were there. Coach Green wouldn't like it if his mind wasn't on the scrimmage they were about to play.

Ty Hendrickson came up alongside Kadeem. He was Southside High's best running back. "Paige says those guys are college scouts. They've had their eyes on you and me all through practice," he said. Paige was Ty's girlfriend, the captain of Southside's cheerleading team.

Kadeem felt his heartbeat quicken but tried not to let that show. "How does she know?"

"Who else could they be?"

Kadeem nodded as he tossed his helmet in his hands. "Okay, so it's finally starting. It's about time."

"I hear you, man," Ty said. "I thought they'd never get around to us."

"And she saw them looking at us?" Kadeem checked.

"That's what she told me." Ty stepped closer and dropped his voice to avoid being overhead. "Come on, who else are they going to be checking out, besides us?"

Kadeem looked around at his teammates.

He decided there were a few other possible candidates who might get recruited by colleges for football scholarships. Norval Lamb was an unstoppable fullback. Arnie Johnson was a fast and fearless tight end. But—putting false modesty aside—Ty was right. Ty and Kadeem were definitely the Titans' two star players.

"I sure hope so," Ty continued. "My old man drank up my college fund years ago. No dough, no go. So a football scholarship is my only shot."

"My folks might have a little college money set aside. I'm not exactly sure," Kadeem agreed. "But my GPA is a little shaky, if you know what I mean."

"For real?" Ty questioned. "I always think of you as a smart guy."

"I didn't get serious about school until the end of last year. And by the second half of junior year, it was kind of too late to build it up," Kadeem said. "Being recruited for football will help. Otherwise I might not have a shot. Plus, I wouldn't mind playing pro football someday. I've got to play college ball first if I'm going to do that."

Ty looked at Kadeem, impressed. "I bet you could do it."

"How about you?" Kadeem asked.

"I don't know if I have the right stuff for pro ball," Ty admitted. "But you do, for sure."

Kadeem sighed deeply. "I hope so."

Ty delivered a good-natured slap to Kadeem's back. "Don't sweat it, man. If anybody's getting an offer from these guys, it'll be you."

Coach Green blew a whistle, marking the end of the break. As Kadeem lined up with his teammates, he took another look at the recruiters. They were walking along the sidelines. No doubt they were coming closer for a better position from which to study the players.

"Jones, your team is on offense," the coach announced.

Cool, Kadeem thought. *I get to show what I can do right at the start. It's my chance to make a great impression.*

Kadeem's shoulders tensed. This was supposed to have been a casual scrimmage. It had suddenly become the most important game Kadeem had played all season.

CHAPTER 2

Touchdown!

With one last effort, the ball crossed the goal line, and Coach Green blasted his whistle, ending the scrimmage.

Kadeem held the football high, pumping it in the air. His cheering teammates surrounded him, slapping helmets and high-fiving. It had only been a scrimmage, but winning always felt good. Kadeem tried to seem unconcerned with the scouts on the sidelines, but he could practically feel their eyes on him.

He had really shone. He'd run for that last touchdown and completed all but three of his passes—and two were touchdown passes! He couldn't have asked for a better showcase of his skills.

"Clean up and meet me in the locker room," Coach Green said. "There are some plays I want to go over."

Kadeem looked around for the scouts but didn't see any of them. Had they all gone home already?

That was too bad. But Kadeem still felt good about his performance as he headed across the blazing hot practice field toward the locker rooms.

"Son? Young man?" Kadeem turned toward the voice. He faced a heavyset, middle-aged man in a green jacket. He wore glasses and was balding. Kadeem thought he recognized the man as one of the scouts. "I'm Frank Harris from Teller University," the man said as he stuck out his hand to shake.

Kadeem shook Frank Harris's hand and introduced himself.

"I know who you are," the man said. "Fantastic job out there just now—really spectacular! You have some arm."

"Thanks," Kadeem said. He worked to keep his voice steady as nervous excitement raced through him. Teller had a legendary football program. Playing for them pretty much guaranteed that he would play in bowl games and be scouted by the pros when the time came.

"Are you doing anything right now?" Frank Harris asked.

"I have to go over some plays with Coach, and then I'm free."

"Care to get a bite to eat with me? I want to tell you about Teller and our program. Do you think you might be interested in playing for us?"

"Sure," Kadeem replied, his voice raspy from nervousness.

"Great! I'll wait for you out here on the bleachers."

Kadeem tried hard to concentrate on what Coach Green was saying during his review of the plays. Then he hurried into the locker room to shower. "I saw the Teller scout talking to you," Ty said, as Kadeem was dressing. "Did you get an offer?"

"Not yet," Kadeem told him. "We're going to get something to eat and talk, though."

"Lucky," Ty said. "Nobody else got that much from Teller. Matt Olsen got approached by a guy from Texas State, and Chris Michaels is talking to the scout from DeWitt U."

Kadeem couldn't help notice Ty's jealousy. "Give it time. I think these are just the first go-sees. These guys will be back," Kadeem said, trying to be hopeful. He hoped they'd be back. "Other scouts from other universities will come, too. These aren't the only ones," he added.

"Yeah, but Teller . . . that's big," Ty mentioned.

Kadeem patted his shoulder. "Hey man, you gotta stay positive. Anyway, I'll tell him I know a great running back."

"Do that!" Ty called to him as Kadeem headed out the locker-room door.

CHAPTER 3

Frank Harris was waiting on the bottom step of the bleachers when Kadeem got there. He drove Kadeem downtown to a restaurant called Mel's Place.

They walked into the restaurant and sat at a table in the back. Frank Harris ordered them each a burger and soda.

"Kadeem, I'm not prepared to make any promises at this point," he said as he sipped his soda. "I have to see you in action more. I need to know what kind of player you really are. But right now I just wanted to get a feel for *who* you are. Tell me, son, what do you know about Teller?"

"I know Teller has a fine football program," Kadeem said. "But to be honest, my grades might not make the cut."

Frank Harris waved his hand. "We can get around that."

"For real?"

"The football program is very, very key at Teller. Wealthy alumni love to have a winning team. They donate big-time to their alma mater when the football team wins. The school administration is well aware of that fact. They're happy to bend the admission rules if it means having a top-notch team on the field every year. Your professors will work with us on that, too."

"Which means?" Kadeem asked, not quite understanding.

"It means you'll be able to handle the course work just fine. They know that you have practices to attend, and Teller doesn't want you to lose your scholarship because of academic difficulties." Frank Harris winked as he said this, and Kadeem got the idea: there would be no chance that he'd fail at Teller. His grades would be guaranteed by his status as a football player.

"So, what do you think? Sound good?" Frank Harris asked.

"Sounds great. And I'd love to go to Teller. But I'll have to weigh all the offers that I might get. I need the biggest possible scholarsh—"

"Hi, Coach Harris!" A female voice interrupted Kadeem. He turned to see a tall, slim girl with curly black hair held back with a thin golden headband.

"Alyssa! What are you doing around here?" Frank Harris asked. "Kadeem, this is Alyssa Watson. She's one of our cheerleaders at Teller."

Alyssa nodded at Kadeem and said to Coach Harris, "Some of the other girls and I are visiting Keah Andrews. She lives around here."

"I know Keah," Kadeem said. "She graduated from Southside a couple of years ago."

"You do? Well, she's right behind me. We're on the Teller cheerleading team together."

"I remember. She was captain of the cheerleading team when I was a sophomore," Kadeem recalled.

"I'm a freshman . . . in college that is," Alyssa told him.

"Cool," he said. She was really pretty, with big dark eyes and a winning smile, not to mention curves in all the right places.

"Keah wouldn't know me," Kadeem added. "I was only a sophomore the year she graduated. I know her because, you know, sophomores always know the juniors and seniors."

Two other very good-looking girls came into the restaurant. Kadeem recognized one as Keah Andrews.

"Kadeem!" Keah cried happily. "How have you been?"

Kadeem smiled. He felt flattered that this college girl remembered him. That she called him by name was completely amazing. The girls pulled out chairs and sat down with Coach Harris and Kadeem.

Frank Harris ordered them all sodas while the three girls told Kadeem how much they loved going to Teller.

"We hear you're doing great things for Southside this year," Keah said. "I always knew you'd be a star."

"I can't believe you remember me," Kadeem admitted.

"Of course I do. You were already playing varsity as a freshman. Everyone was talking about you."

"Really?" Kadeem was now amazed and flattered.

"Sure," Keah said.

"You actually played varsity as a freshman? Wow!" Alyssa said. "Impressive. No wonder you're the captain now." She looked at Frank Harris. "Coach, Teller could really use a guy like Kadeem."

"Well, we'll see," Frank Harris said.

Kadeem couldn't get enough of all the attention. It felt great. And the attention from Alyssa, in particular, made him smile.

CHAPTER 4

That night, Kadeem sat on his bed with his laptop. He tapped the side of it, deep in thought.

Before leaving Mel's Place, he'd gotten Alyssa's e-mail address. He'd given her his e-mail and added his cell phone number as well. Was it too soon to contact her? Would he seem like some overly eager, geeky high-school kid if he got in touch within hours of meeting her?

Kadeem didn't like feeling so unsure of himself. He was the captain of the football team, after all. He knew lots of girls liked him.

Usually, he was cool around the girls in school. But Alyssa was in college. He didn't want her to think he was a love-struck kid.

He went to Facebook and searched for her. Her profile came up right away. He studied her photo. She was so hot!

"She likes me," he said, thinking aloud. "She wouldn't have given me her contact stuff if she didn't." He clicked the friend button.

Kadeem waited, hoping for an immediate reply. After nearly ten minutes more, he began to despair. He'd just have to wait until she checked her friend requests.

He had her e-mail address. He could use it. But he decided that sending an e-mail and a friend request at the same time appeared a little too desperate. And that was the last thing he wanted to seem.

Kadeem heard his home phone ring but ignored it. His friends called only on his cell. It stopped after two rings. Then his father called from the living room. "Kadeem! It's for you."

Laying his laptop aside, Kadeem swung his legs over the side of the bed. Who would be calling him on the house phone? He hurried to the living room, worrying that it might be a teacher or some other kind of trouble.

His father read the concern in Kadeem's eyes as he handed his son the cordless phone. It seemed to amuse him. "Relax," he advised Kadeem. "It's a Coach Harris from Teller."

What did Frank Harris want so soon?

"Hello?" Kadeem said. "Coach Harris?"

"Kadeem, on the way home I had a thought. Teller is playing Peterson this Saturday. Would you like to come see the game? I've invited some of your teammates who also interest us. They're all coming. What do you say?"

"Sure. It sounds like fun!" Kadeem agreed. "Thanks."

"Great! You'll have a blast. I'll come by for you on Saturday morning. Maybe we'll catch some breakfast first. Oh, and by the way, the girls you met today will be cheering at the game."

"Alyssa?" Kadeem couldn't resist asking.

Frank Harris chuckled. "I could tell you liked her," he said. "She's a great gal. Yeah, I imagine she'll be there with the other cheerleaders."

The first thing Kadeem did when he returned to his room was to check Facebook. There was still no word from Alyssa.

CHAPTER 5

C atch these seats," Ty commented to Kadeem as they made their way down to seats that were right on the sidelines of the Peterson University football field.

"I know. First class," Kadeem replied.

"Man, I can't believe I got invited to this," Ty said.

"I told you it would happen," Kadeem said as they took their seats. He turned and waved to Frank Harris, who was coming down the aisle with two other players from the Titans, Norval Lamb and Arnie Johnson.

Frank Harris had also invited three players from Northside High. Kadeem knew the Northside guys from previous games. One was a fullback, the other one was a center. The third was the team captain.

Kadeem realized he had been Frank Harris's only pick for quarterback. That was a good sign for him.

The Teller cheerleaders came out and faced the audience. Scanning their faces, Kadeem quickly found Alyssa. Why hadn't she responded to his Facebook friend request or the e-mail he had sent her two days later? Was it possible that she didn't like him? She had seemed to be interested when she gave him her information. He felt let down.

The cheerleaders launched into their routine. It was led by Keah Andrews. Kadeem wondered if he'd have a chance to speak to Alyssa later.

He'd have to try.

It might be his only chance to ever speak to her again—unless, of course, he attended Teller the following year. Despite the fact that Alyssa appeared to be blowing him off, he couldn't stop thinking about her.

The game began, and it was close at the start. Teller's offense and defense were strong, but so were Peterson's. By halftime, though, Teller had a solid lead.

During halftime, Coach Harris gave each of them a twenty-dollar bill to buy themselves some lunch. He'd already treated them to a full breakfast before the game.

Kadeem had just bought a foot-long hot dog at the stand when a stocky man with red hair and ruddy skin approached him. His jacket was the deep blue of the Peterson Pirates.

"Hello, Kadeem," he said, sticking out his hand to shake. "I'm Roy Fellows, assistant coach for the Pirates."

"Hi," Kadeem replied. He shook the man's hand. "How do you know my name?"

Roy Fellows smiled. "I was at your practice the other day. I asked about you. I was impressed, but Frank Harris was taking up all your time, so we didn't get to talk. Any chance you'd be interested in playing for Peterson?"

"It depends on what Peterson has to offer," Kadeem replied. Kadeem told him that he needed as big a scholarship as possible.

"How are your grades?" Roy Fellows asked.

"Borderline," Kadeem admitted.

"Hmmm," Roy Fellows mused. "Any chance you could still bring them up this year?"

His words surprised Kadeem. He'd expected that Roy Fellows would tell him the same thing Frank Harris had—not to worry about it. Kadeem suddenly felt annoyed. Who was this guy from the losing Peterson team to tell him to get his grades up?

"I'll try," Kadeem said without enthusiasm. "Teller has already told me not to worry about it."

Roy Fellows's eyebrows shot up. "They have?"

"Yeah, and they've taken me out to eat. They've also introduced me to some of their cheerleaders, and brought me and some of the guys to this game. This hot dog I'm eating was paid for by Coach Harris. He's buying us dinner on the way home, too."

"Oh, really?" Roy Fellows said. "He introduced you to the cheerleaders, eh?"

"Well, yeah. I guess they just happened to be there, but he invited them to sit with us."

"I see. Well, don't expect Peterson to be doing all that," Roy Fellows commented.

"Then, no offense, but it seems like Peterson is not that interested in having me play for them," Kadeem said. As he heard his own words, Kadeem knew he sounded a bit arrogant. But those were the facts as he saw them. Teller was making a big deal over him and Peterson wasn't.

Looking over the Peterson coach's shoulder, Kadeem spied Alyssa. She was in line at a food stand. "Excuse me," he said, dashing away from Roy Fellows. "Nice talking to you." If the coach said anything else, Kadeem didn't hear it. His attention was already on someone else.

—— —— —— —— ——

"Hey," Kadeem said, coming alongside Alyssa as she stood in the line.

"Hi," Alyssa replied. "Hey, listen, I need to talk to you. The reason I didn't get back to you is . . . well, it's a little embarrassing. My boyfriend Alex is a real jealous type, and he knows my passwords. He's graduating early in January, though. I plan on breaking up with him then."

"Oh, that's good," Kadeem said. In fact, it was great. He should have known that a pretty girl like Alyssa would already have a boyfriend. But since he was about to graduate, it was perfect.

"Hey, let me buy you whatever you're having. It's on Coach Harris, actually. He gave us cash for lunch."

"Thanks. Next year, we can do this all the time. That is, if you come to Teller," Alyssa said, smiling up at him.

"We could," Kadeem agreed. Over Alyssa's shoulder, Kadeem could see that coach from Peterson frowning in the distance. He didn't focus on him, though. Teller was looking better and better every minute.

CHAPTER 6

The Titans' next home game was against Northside. Kadeem didn't notice Alyssa in the stands until it was nearly time for kickoff. She was there with Keah Andrews and other girls from the Teller cheerleading team. He squinted across the sunny field. They were each holding something. Were they signs?

"Check it," Ty said, jogging up to him. "Your dream girl is here. She's holding a sign that reads 'Come to Teller, Kadeem!'"

"What!?" Kadeem cried. "You're joking me."

"No. Look!"

Moving at a casual jog, Kadeem went closer to the girls.

"Kadeem!" Alyssa shouted, waving.

She really had a dynamite smile.

Alyssa pointed excitedly to her sign. Kadeem responded with a thumbs-up.

Kadeem waved to Alyssa. He waved to his parents, who were sitting on the fifty-yard line. Kadeem then made his way to the thirty-five-yard line. He waited for his teammates to get ready for kickoff.

Kadeem got into position. He called the plays and received the snap from the center. Kadeem quickly handed the ball off to Ty.

Ty raced forward for five yards before a Nomad defensive end contained him just beyond the line of scrimmage. Pivoting quickly, Ty lateralled the ball back to Kadeem.

Kadeem caught the pass and put his head down to barrel his way toward the end zone.

A Northside player was gaining on him,

but Norval made the block. Kadeem sprinted and zigzagged past the other players and somersaulted into the end zone.

Touchdown!

Kadeem had scored the first touchdown of the game.

The Southside fans cheered loudly. Kadeem spied Alyssa in the bleachers, waving her sign.

For the rest of the game, all Kadeem could think about was that Alyssa was watching him. He was off to a great start, but he had to keep looking good for her. This made him faster and more alert than ever as he escaped sack after sack and passed for four more touchdowns. He was playing at the top of his game, and he knew it.

Everyone could see it.

Each time the team scored, the Titan fans went wild in the bleachers. A nearly deafening roar arose from the stands. Alyssa was seeing him at his best. Imagining what she was thinking just made Kadeem play better.

At the end of the game, the Titans had

won by several TDs. His teammates scooped Kadeem onto their shoulders. They carried him around as far as the door to the school locker rooms, chanting, "Ka-DEEM! Ka-DEEM!"

Kadeem's mother and father were there waiting for him. "That's my boy!" his father said, slapping Kadeem on the back. "You've made your old man proud."

"Thanks, Dad."

"Do you need a ride home?" his mother asked.

"No thanks. We're going out to celebrate. I'll catch you later."

As his parents turned to leave, he saw Alyssa.

"Woo-hooo! Way to go, Kadeem!" she cheered with a small jump and fist pump. "You were awesome!"

"Hey! Thanks for coming to the game. Are you at Keah's place again? I'm sure you didn't come all this way just to see this game."

"I did," Alyssa said.

"Did what?" Kadeem asked.

"Come to see you."

Kadeem gave Alyssa a skeptical glance. "You did not."

"It seemed like a good way to see you again without Alex finding out." Alyssa looked a little embarrassed. "Are you going out with your team after your win?"

"Yeah, want to come?"

"I'd rather go out alone, just me and you," Alyssa said.

Had he heard her right? For a second, Kadeem wasn't sure. "Just you and me?" he checked.

"I'm sorry," Alyssa said, turning away from him. "I know you want to be with your team. I just thought that maybe—"

"No . . . no," Kadeem cut her off. "I can see those guys any time. I'd much rather be with you."

Alyssa turned back to him, smiling. "I'm happy that's how you feel."

Kadeem wasn't sure what gave him the nerve. The moment just felt right. He leaned down for a kiss.

Alyssa reached her arms around his shoulders and kissed his lips. It was everything he had been dreaming of. His future was falling into place—a potential scholarship to Teller... Alyssa ... everything.

CHAPTER 7

Where were you last night?" Ty asked the next day at practice. They were in line to run through a course of car tires that had been set up on the field. "I kept waiting for you to show."

"I went out with Alyssa," Kadeem replied.

"Oooooh," Ty teased knowingly. "It's like that, is it?"

Kadeem just grinned in response. As the drill line moved forward, he noticed two men he had never seen before walking toward the field. One was in a deep blue jacket, and the other wore a green baseball cap. "More scouts, do you think?" Kadeem asked, poking Ty and nodding toward the men.

"I sure hope so. Nobody's made me an offer yet. How about you?"

"Not yet, but I'm pretty sure Teller is going to come through. Peterson talked to me, but they're being a pain in the butt over grades. I'd rather go to Teller anyway," admitted Kadeem.

Peering through the sunlight, Kadeem realized he did recognize one of the men. "That guy there is the one I spoke to from Peterson," he told Ty. "His name is Roy Fellows. I don't know the man with him, though."

With a nod, Ty ran onto the tires, making his way down the line. Kadeem was right behind him. When Kadeem came out the other side, his heart pounded from the effort.

For the next hour, the men stood on the sidelines. They watched Kadeem run through

all the practice drills. As he was leaving
the field, they approached him. "Hi there,
Kadeem. Can we talk to you for a moment?"
Roy Fellows asked.

"Sure," Kadeem agreed, feeling uneasy.
These guys looked so serious. What was up?

"This is Alan Murphy from the National
Collegiate Athletic Association," Roy Fellows
introduced the tall man at his side. Kadeem
noticed that Alan Murphy's baseball cap bore
the initials NCAA. Kadeem knew that the
NCAA governed the nation's college and
university athletic programs. What did they
want with him?

"Hello, Kadeem," Alan Murphy said and
extended his hand. "Mr. Fellows has brought
it to my attention that you recently informed
him of recruitment violations on the part of
Teller University."

Alarms went off in Kadeem's head. What
was this guy talking about?

"I did?" he asked Roy Fellows. "I don't
think so."

"Yes, you did. It was the other day at the

Teller versus Peterson game. Remember? We talked about the money, the pretty girls, the free tickets, the waiving of grade requirements," Roy Fellows reminded him.

"Those are recruitment violations?" Kadeem asked.

"Yes, they are," Alan Murphy confirmed. "And we've been informed that cheerleaders from Teller were at your last game. They held signs urging you and a few other players to sign up with Teller."

"Yeah, they were there. What's wrong with that?" Kadeem asked.

"There are limitations on how many times a scout can visit each player. Teller likes to get around that by sending cheerleaders to high-school football games. Pretty girls make good salespeople when young men are deciding where to go to college."

Kadeem's head was spinning as he took in this news. Did that mean that Alyssa hadn't attended the game because she wanted to see him? Had she really come because the coaches at Teller had sent her? Had she spent time

43

with him—and even kissed him—just for that reason? He didn't believe it.

"Those girls came because they're friends," Kadeem objected.

"Really?" Alan Murphy said skeptically. "And how long have you known these friends?"

"Not long," Kadeem admitted. "I met them through Coach . . . " His voice trailed off as he realized what Alan Murphy was implying.

"You met them through Assistant Coach Harris of Teller," Roy Fellows recapped for Kadeem.

"Right," Kadeem agreed. He shook his head sadly.

It couldn't be true. Alyssa really seemed to be into him.

"Kadeem, it's pretty clear to us that Teller wants you to play for them," Alan Murphy said. "Teller has a great team. But one of the reasons Teller is so successful in attracting the best players is that they don't play by the recruitment rules."

"Okay, I get it," Kadeem said cautiously. He wished he hadn't stopped to talk to these guys. The picture he had in his head of Alyssa and him happily walking hand in hand across the Teller campus was becoming blurry. He didn't like it one bit.

CHAPTER 8

All the way home Kadeem felt like he was riding an emotional roller coaster. First he was worried and confused. Then he felt betrayed and hurt. How could Alyssa be so cold? Slowly, though, toward the end of the bus ride home, he had become angry—really angry!

As Kadeem walked into his apartment, he wondered why they had to pick on him. Couldn't they have chosen someone else to be their snitch? He didn't want to be some kind of undercover agent for the NCAA. But that was exactly what they had asked him to do. Alan Murphy wanted Kadeem to go along with the Teller recruitment process and keep a record of everything that was said and done. Kadeem was supposed to keep this record until he received a definite offer to play for them. Then he was supposed to give his record to Alan Murphy.

Kadeem pounded his fist on the counter. He didn't want Teller busted for recruitment violations. He wanted to go to school there! He wanted to play quarterback for the Teller team! If he ratted them out, there would be no chance they'd offer him a football scholarship.

It wasn't fair!

Why had he blabbed to that Roy Fellows? "You idiot!" Kadeem mumbled, blaming himself. It had been sheer pride that had made him boast about what Teller was doing to recruit him. And now his pride had gotten him into a mess.

Kadeem's cell phone buzzed. He took it from the pocket of his jeans. He didn't recognize the caller-ID number, but after another ring he answered it anyway. "Kadeem! Glad I reached you," the voice on the other end spoke.

It was Frank Harris. He invited Kadeem to spend the upcoming weekend at Teller. He'd be going along with Ty, Norval Lamb, and Arnie Johnson. "We can leave tomorrow after class and stay through Sunday morning. You'll see the campus and get the feel of it," Frank Harris explained. "What do you say? Can you make it?"

"Sure," Kadeem answered. Normally he'd have been really jazzed to go, but now he wasn't so sure.

"You okay?" Frank Harris asked. "You sound out of it."

"No, no," Kadeem lied. "Everything's fine. I guess I'm a little tired from practice."

"I can understand that. No pain, no gain," Frank Harris said. "Okay, I'll be in touch. Glad you can make it."

Kadeem sat at the table, drumming his fingers pensively. Alan Murphy had told him that recruiting coaches were allowed only one phone call a month to possible recruits. Kadeem brought up the record of incoming calls on his cell phone: ten calls from Frank Harris in just two weeks. That alone was not good.

Kadeem's phone buzzed again. This time, he recognized Ty's number on the caller ID. "We're going to Teller, man!" Ty shouted excitedly. "We are in! Why else would we be invited?"

A knot was forming in Kadeem's stomach. If Teller was busted for recruitment violations, how would that affect all the other guys who were being recruited? Would they be blamed? Would they lose any chance at an athletic scholarship? "Maybe you shouldn't go," Kadeem suggested.

"What? Are you nuts?"

"Doesn't it seem to you that Teller is going overboard in their recruitment?" Kadeem pointed out to Ty. "Maybe we should be looking at other schools besides Teller."

"You don't think I can make it into Teller?" Ty asked. There was an edge of anger in his voice.

"It isn't that. They just make me a little nervous. I think they might be in violation of some recruitment rules."

There! He had said it. Now Ty couldn't blame him if there were problems later.

"What? Kadeem, man, who cares?" Ty replied with a scornful laugh. "I'm not telling anybody . . . are you?"

"Maybe I will."

"Yeah, sure," Ty scoffed. "And pass up a chance to get a free ride? I don't think so."

Kadeem inhaled deeply and let it out slowly. "No, I guess not."

"You have that right," Ty agreed. "Come on, it's going to be great. They'll throw free stuff at us. You'll get to hang with that Alyssa chick you're hot for. Too bad I'm with Paige now. I wouldn't mind hanging out with some college babe."

Kadeem spoke to Ty for a while longer before hanging up. He wished he could roll back time to the Peterson versus Teller game. If he could live it over again, he'd keep his big mouth shut.

"Hungry?" his mother asked, coming into the kitchen carrying a bag of groceries.

"A little," Kadeem admitted as he got up to help his mother with the groceries. "When's Dad getting home?" he asked.

His mother began putting away the food. "Not until tomorrow. He's in the firehouse today. He switched with someone. Can I help with something? Is something on your mind, Kadeem?"

His mother just wouldn't understand like his father would. Kadeem's dad had played football in college.

"Nah, I'm fine. Can I go to Teller for the weekend with some guys?"

After he had answered a dozen questions about the trip to her satisfaction, Kadeem's mother gave her permission. "You don't seem very enthused about it," she noted.

"Oh, I am," Kadeem answered listlessly. "I'm just tired." He was tired—tired of this whole business.

CHAPTER 9

K adeem sat up front with Frank Harris as they drove out of town toward Teller. Arnie Simon and Norval Lamb were in the back. Arnie was staring at his PSP, and Norval's head was tipped back with his cap over his eyes. He snored softly.

"What happened to Ty?" Frank Harris asked.

"His dad is driving him because he couldn't leave with us after school.

Some make-up test or something," Kadeem said.

The traffic was heavy, but they reached Teller in about two hours. It was already dark, but the campus was well lit. Gray stone buildings with gargoyles along the rooftops lined winding paths. Around the buildings, students sat talking on benches around perfectly manicured lawns. It was just like Kadeem had pictured it, and it was very easy for him to imagine himself in this setting next year.

Later that night, they watched a home game: Teller versus Miller College. The game was fun to watch but not very suspenseful, since Teller came out strong in the first half and continued to score touchdown after touchdown throughout the second. Kadeem was impressed with their offensive strategies and the skills exhibited by several of their players. It would be a dream come true to play for a team like Teller.

Kadeem watched Alyssa down on the

field, cheering and jumping along with the other cheerleaders. Just because she was trying to encourage him to attend Teller didn't mean she had no feelings for him, right? She might have originally been working for the interests of Teller, but somewhere along the line, she had become genuinely attracted to him. He at least owed her the benefit of the doubt. She could be for real.

"We're having a little event for you guys over at the faculty lounge," Frank Harris told him. "Your favorite cheerleader will be there," he added with a wink.

"Cool," Kadeem answered.

"Are you all right, kid? You seem a little . . . I don't know . . . lacking in enthusiasm," Frank Harris remarked.

"Naw, practices have just been hard." Kadeem tried to explain away his nervousness. The truth was that he was depressed. Teller had everything that he wanted for himself, and now he couldn't have it . . . unless, of course, he lied.

Maybe there was another way. He could tell Frank Harris everything. Together, they could concoct a story to tell the NCAA. He could say he came to Teller on his own to look around. He could tell them that Alyssa and he had met online and hit it off, and that was why she came to see him. He could deny ever having told Roy Fellows those things. Frank Harris could claim that Roy Fellows was just saying these things to get Kadeem to play for Peterson.

Kadeem had that feeling that all quarterbacks know: His offensive line was crumbling. He had to decide what to do with the ball before the defense crushed him.

"Something on your mind?" Frank Harris asked, sensing Kadeem's growing agitation as this plan formed in his head.

"No, just thinking about stuff," Kadeem covered. He wasn't ready to confide in the Teller coach . . . not yet.

"Come on, let's walk over to the Faculty Lounge," Frank Harris suggested. "You need a little food and drink in you. It's been a long day."

The lounge was set up with tables abundantly spread with all sorts of food. There was a bar that served soda and alcohol. A sign read "You Must Be 21." But Kadeem saw Arnie and Norval with bottles of beer in their hands.

"Have you guys seen Ty?" Kadeem asked when he joined them.

"I just called him. His old man was supposed to drive him, but something went wrong. He's coming by bus now—he's getting Paige to take him to the bus station," Norval replied.

Members of the Teller team began to stroll in slowly. They piled their plates high with food and then approached Kadeem, Norval, and Arnie. "You guys won't be sorry if you pick Teller," one of them said.

Kadeem recognized him as number four. "Awesome game," he complimented the linebacker. "Great intercept in the first quarter."

The guys started analyzing the different plays and scenarios. Kadeem was interested, but he always had one eye on the door, waiting for Alyssa to arrive. "Excuse me," he said the moment she appeared, still in her cheerleading outfit.

"Hi, Kadeem," she said with that lovely smile that lit him up. "What did you think of the game?"

"Amazing offense," Kadeem replied. "Is your jealous boyfriend around?"

Alyssa shook her ahead. "He went home this weekend."

"Good," Kadeem said. "Listen, I need to talk to you. Do you think we can get out of here?"

Before Alyssa could answer, Frank Harris was at their side, reaching into his wallet. "Why don't you kids go out later," he said, pulling a fifty out and offering it to Kadeem. "Have some fun—it's on me."

"We were just talking about leaving, but Alyssa hasn't told me if she wants to yet," Kadeem said.

"Okay, but could you pick me up at my sorority house in about a half hour, Kadeem? I need to change."

"Sure thing," Kadeem said. "We can talk then." The only problem was that Kadeem had no idea what to say to her.

CHAPTER 10

K adeem waited on the porch of Alyssa's off-campus sorority house. It was a huge, Victorian-style building on a tidy residential street. She had been inside more than twenty minutes, and he was beginning to get impatient.

As Kadeem sat rocking lightly on the porch swing, his phone rang, and he recognized the number. It was Alan Murphy for the NCAA. For a second, Kadeem considered not picking up, but at the last moment he answered.

"Hi, Kadeem. Am I catching you at a good time? Where are you?" Alan Murphy asked.

"Ah, nowhere," Kadeem lied. "Home, I mean."

"Well, have you decided if you're willing to help us out?"

"Uh, not yet. Could I have another day to think about it?"

"Of course. But I hope you decide to do the right thing," Alan Murphy said. "It *is* the right thing to do, Kadeem."

"Okay, well, I'll let you know, okay?" he replied.

Where was Alyssa? He intended to talk to her honestly about this whole recruitment violation business. What she said in response would be the deciding factor in his decision.

Standing, Kadeem decided to go in. He entered the house's spacious front hall and spied Alyssa in a room to the right. He was about to tell her to hurry up when he realized she was talking to someone on her cell phone.

He held back to give her a moment to finish talking.

"I can't wait for all this recruitment stuff to be over," Alyssa said. "It is so boring hanging out with high-school guys. Soon I can spend more time with you guys and Kenny again."

Alyssa turned around and saw Kadeem.

Mortified and hurt, Kadeem stormed out of the hall and down the steps. How could he have been such an idiot? He had never felt more foolish in his life.

CHAPTER 11

Kadeem was exhausted by the time he walked into his apartment on Sunday night. He had gone to a Teller practice and even participated. Then there had been a tour of the campus and another dinner.

Alyssa had called and texted him all weekend, but he had ignored her. When she showed up at breakfast in the cafeteria Sunday morning, he wouldn't even look her way. When she came toward him, he moved.

Finally, she had given up and gone away.

"How was it, Kadeem?" his father asked when Kadeem stepped into the kitchen.

"Not great," Kadeem said, taking a seat at the kitchen table across from his father.

Kadeem's father put down the newspaper he had been reading. "Want to talk about it?" he offered.

"Yeah, Dad, I do." Kadeem told his father everything that had been happening.

"Son, that's quite a situation you're in," was all his father could say at first.

"What should I do, Dad? I want to do the right thing, but I don't want to blow my chance to go to Teller," Kadeem confessed. "What if it makes the other scouts stay away from me, too?"

Kadeem's father rubbed his forehead and sighed. "This makes me think of when I was playing high-school football," he said. "There was this one time when some guys on the team got mixed up in a betting scheme. They planned to throw the game for a cut of the bet money."

"You weren't involved in it, were you?" Kadeem asked.

"No, but I knew about it, and I didn't say anything."

"You couldn't rat out your teammates."

"I should have," his father disagreed. "My team lost a big game because of those guys. I mean, we got *whipped*. As a result, several college scouts passed on players they had been looking at. A few of my teammates missed their chance to go to college and maybe play pro ball. Some of those guys got into some nasty stuff afterward. One of them got into dealing and died of a drug overdose before he was twenty."

"It wasn't your fault," Kadeem insisted.

"Maybe . . . maybe not. The question has bothered me for a long time. I still wonder about it. If I had turned those guys in, would life have been different for those other players?"

"So what are you saying, Dad?" Kadeem asked.

"That sometimes we have to do the hard thing because it's the right thing to do," his father answered. He got up from the table and patted Kadeem on the shoulder. "It's a hard decision, Son. Why don't you sleep on it?"

"I will. Thanks, Dad."

"Goodnight, Kadeem."

Kadeem remained, tapping the edges of the kitchen table thoughtfully. He didn't need to sleep on it. Reaching for his cell phone, he found Alan Murphy's number and hit call.

CHAPTER 12

The next game the Titans would play was against the Uniondale Cougars. It would decide which team went to the play-offs. Southside High was in a fever of excitement, with posters all over the school.

After lunch on the day of the game, Kadeem checked in with Alan Murphy by cell phone. "Remember, we can't charge them with any violation until they make you an official offer," Alan Murphy advised.

"So continue to look like everything's fine. But the minute you get a solid offer from them, call me. You have to get something in writing."

"Okay," Kadeem agreed and said good-bye.

"Hey, man," Ty greeted him. "Ready for tonight?"

"I guess so," said Kadeem. "But you look really tense. What's going on?"

"Just nervous, I guess," Ty admitted. "A lot's riding on this. If Harris is there tonight, I bet he's going to make some decisions."

"Think so?" Kadeem asked.

Ty nodded. "I haven't been able to sleep all week thinking about it. I really want to go to Teller."

"You've got to chill a little," Kadeem advised Ty. "There are other schools besides Teller."

"Not for me. I'm sold on Teller."

"I'm just saying," Kadeem insisted, "there *are* other schools."

That night, the game was in Uniondale. It was clear and cold, and the lights were so bright that they wiped out any view of the stars above.

The stands were packed on both sides, and the atmosphere was electric with excitement. Kadeem located his parents on the bleachers and waved. His father shot him a thumbs-up, and his mother blew him a kiss. Kadeem also spied Frank Harris. Not far away from him were Alan Murphy and Roy Fellows. He also noticed other scouts he had seen at practices. Clearly, a lot more than the chance to move on to the play-offs was riding on this game.

In the huddle, Kadeem called the play. When he received the ball, the Cougar defensive line came at him with all they had. Seeing that Ty was open, Kadeem threw the ball to him just a moment before he was sacked. Jumping high to catch the pass, Ty ran with it.

The Cougar defense was instantly after Ty. Kadeem was up again and watching. He could see that Ty was about to go down. Why didn't he throw a lateral to Norval? He was open! Kadeem knew why. Ty was showing off for the scouts in the stands. He had forgotten one of the first rules of football: use the ball, don't let the ball use you.

Despite Ty's grandstanding, the rest of the team played well, particularly Kadeem. *Forget about the scouts*, he told himself. *Forget all of it; just concentrate on the game.* With this in mind, he was able to focus and threw completion after completion and two touchdown passes. At halftime, the score was tied.

The Cougars and the Titans remained neck and neck throughout the second half, and the game went into overtime. The fans in the bleachers roared with excitement at each down.

The Cougars scored a field goal, and their side went wild.

The Titans had four downs to score or they'd be done.

The Cougars managed to contain Ty and Kadeem for the first three downs. Kadeem could barely contain his frustration at being the object of the entire Cougar defense. But as angry as he felt, Kadeem could see that Ty was even more distressed by it. At one point, as Ty got to his feet after being tackled, he slammed his right fist into his left palm. Kadeem had seen him make this gesture before. It always meant Ty was about to lose his cool. And when Ty's temper erupted, the guy didn't think straight—which meant he made questionable judgments on the field.

Ty couldn't afford to play badly tonight. Not only were the play-offs at stake, but the stands were filled with college football scouts. Ty hadn't played that well when they were at Teller. Maybe tonight he would impress a different coach. He might still have a shot at an offer.

With their season on the line, Kadeem threw a short pass to Ty, who leaped into the air and snagged the ball over the head of a defender. *Way to go, Ty! Nice catch!* Kadeem thought as he ran down the field along with his teammates. Maybe Ty had gotten it together, and he wouldn't have to worry about him after all.

As Ty raced off with the ball, a couple of teammates blocked the Cougars who came after him. *Go! Go! Go, Ty!* Kaddem cheered silently. But in the next minute, he tensed as several Cougar defenders broke through and gained on Ty.

Ty was their fastest player. If anyone could outrun these guys, it was Ty.

Kadeem saw Ty look into the stands as he ran. Was he nuts? What was he looking for that could be more important than the game?

With a jolt, Kadeem realized what Ty was searching for—scouts! He had the ball, and he couldn't resist checking to see if the college recruiters were watching.

Ty juked left and dodged right as he muscled toward the end zone. The moments of distraction had broken his concentration just enough to allow the Cougar defense to catch him. With only a couple yards to go, Ty was dragging two defenders.

What was the guy doing? Why wasn't Ty running out-of-bounds? There was no way he could get anywhere with those Cougars on him like that. Did he really think he'd make it to the end zone?

Kadeem gritted his teeth in anger. Ty was showing off for the scouts! Kadeem was sure of it now.

A third Cougar hit Ty hard, and he went down at the one-yard line. Even worse, he lost the ball as he hit the ground.

The Cougars had won!

Kadeem hung his head, his shoulders slumped with defeat. When they won, it was as a team, and this time they had lost as a team. He'd try not to be angry at Ty. In a way, it wasn't even his fault. All this recruiting stuff had thrown him off his game.

CHAPTER 13

Kadeem and Ty were the last two in the locker room. They finished getting dressed in silence. Kadeem could see from the dark expression on Ty's face that he blamed himself for the team's defeat. And it was true—in a way. But things happen, and there was no sense saying anything to Ty. If he tried to make Ty feel better it would sound false, and there was no point in making him feel worse. So Kadeem said nothing.

The Southside pep squad was throwing a party in their school cafeteria, win or lose. Kadeem wasn't really up for it, but he was famished, and there would be food.

Outside the locker room, Paige, Ty's cheerleader girlfriend, waited for Ty to come out. "What's taking him so long?" she asked.

Kadeem explained to her that Ty was taking the defeat hard, blaming himself. He shouted inside for Ty to get a move on. Uniondale was going to lock up soon. "And you don't want to miss the Better Luck Next Year party. Free food, man! You can drown your sorrows in ginger ale." He turned back to Paige. "He's coming. See you over there."

"Thanks," Paige replied with a wave as Kadeem went out the back door. The moment Kadeem stepped out, Frank Harris approached.

Reaching into the pocket of his varsity jacket, Kadeem clicked on the small tape recorder Alan Murphy had given him. "You were great out there tonight, Kadeem," Frank Harris said.

"We lost," Kadeem pointed out.

"You can thank your pal Ty for that, but you were on fire. Teller wants you to play for them. How does a three-fourths scholarship for tuition and full room and board sound to you?"

It sounded awesome, and Kadeem ran his fingers along the recorder in his pocket, sorely tempted to switch it off. But he inhaled deeply for strength and let it run.

"Could I have something in writing?" Kadeem requested, remembering that Alan Murphy had told him to get it.

"What? My word isn't good enough?" Frank Harris objected, obviously insulted.

"It isn't that. I just need something to show my parents. I have to talk to them about it."

"Whatever," Frank Harris said dismissively. "I'll see what I can get you."

"Thanks," Kadeem said without emotion.

"Well?" Frank Harris asked.

"Well what?"

"How about a little excitement, some gratitude, something?"

"Yeah, well, thanks. I appreciate the offer. I'll feel excited once it's definite, I guess," Kadeem said.

"I sure hope so," Frank Harris mumbled as he turned to leave—let down by Kadeem's lack of enthusiasm.

The moment Frank Harris was out of sight, Alan Murphy approached Kadeem.

"Well?" Murphy asked. "Did he make an offer?"

"Yes, but not in writing," Kadeem replied. "I have it on tape, though," he added, taking the recorder from his pocket and shutting it off.

Alan Murphy took the tape recorder from him. "Good enough," he said. "When we combine this with the report you're writing up, we can nail him."

CHAPTER 14

Kadeem sat beside his father on a bench outside a closed door. They were at the local headquarters of the NCAA. "Calm down, Kadeem," his father said. "It will be all right. You haven't done anything wrong. You aren't on trial. All you have to do is go in and tell the panel the truth about what happened."

"I know... I know." Kadeem curled his right hand into a fist and punched it into his left palm repeatedly. "I just wish it was over."

A man with a portable TV camera on his shoulder came into the room with another man. Both wore jackets emblazoned with the name of the local TV network.

"You're filming this?" Kadeem asked, suddenly feeling his stomach twist.

"Hey, are you Kadeem Jones?" said the reporter without the camera. "I'm Hank Rosen. I do the sports segment for Channel 39 News. Can I ask you a few questions?"

The cameraman aimed his camera at Kadeem.

"Not now, guys," Kadeem's father stopped them. "He'll make his statement to the NCAA panel. And that's all he'll have to say."

"Suit yourself," Hank Rosen grumbled.

Kadeem's mouth went dry, and he wondered if he'd be able to speak at all. Having these reporters around was making him more nervous. Would Frank Harris be there? How would he ever face him?

Roy Fellows came out the door. "They want you now, Kadeem," he said.

Kadeem and his father got up and went

into a boardroom with a wall of windows and a long table in the middle. Three men and two women sat at the far end of the table. Alan Murphy was at the head. Frank Harris was there, too, sitting several chairs away from the others.

"Have a seat, Kadeem, Mr. Jones," Alan Murphy said pleasantly. "Anywhere you'd like." As he sat, Kadeem tried not to look at Frank Harris, but he could feel the man's angry eyes boring into him.

"Kadeem, the board would like to officially thank you for your help with this matter," Alan Murphy said. "We just have a few questions to ask you, for the record, and then you're free to go."

From the corner of his eye, Kadeem saw the Channel 39 reporter and his cameraman enter the room and take a spot in the corner. His mouth felt even drier, and he wished they weren't there. He nodded to Alan Murphy. "Go ahead," he said, his voice coming out in a croak.

There were a pitcher of water and some paper cups on the table. One of the men on the panel poured a cup and handed it to Kadeem. "Thanks," Kadeem said.

"Did Frank Harris from Teller ever take you out to eat?" asked Alan Murphy.

"Yes," Kadeem replied.

"How many times did he come to see you play last month?"

"Three or four."

"Did he ever call you on your personal phone?" Alan Murphy continued.

"Yes," Kadeem answered.

"How many times?"

"Eight or nine."

"I did not!" Frank Harris yelled, rising slightly from his seat.

Kadeem took out his cell phone and checked the incoming calls in his phone records. "Sorry," he said, "it was twelve times."

"May we see your phone?" Alan Murphy requested.

Kadeem slid it down the table to him. The panel looked at the list of calls and wrote notes on their pads. They went on to ask Kadeem about the weekend at Teller. They wanted to know if alcohol was ever offered, and Kadeem told them that some of the high-school players were drinking. They wanted to know if Frank Harris had ever given him money, and Kadeem recalled the fifty-dollar bill he had been given to "go have a good time" with Alyssa. "But I tried to return it the next day because we never went out," he explained. "Mr. Harris wouldn't take it back, though."

"I was trying to be nice," Frank Harris growled. "That's gratitude for you."

"Why didn't you go on the date?" Alan Murphy asked Kadeem.

Kadeem answered, "Because I overheard a phone call and learned that the girl I was going to go out with was just going with me as a recruitment tactic."

"Did the girl offer you sex?"

"No," Kadeem replied.

"Did you like her?" Alan Murphy asked.

"Yes, I liked her a lot, and I had thought she liked me."

"Would you have gone to Teller so the

two of you could be together?" Alan Murphy pressed.

"Yes," Kadeem admitted.

"Did she tell you she'd be interested in dating you if you went?"

"Yes," said Kadeem, and he sighed.

Alan Murphy slapped his yellow pad with satisfaction. "Thank you, Kadeem. That's all we need. You can go."

Kadeem and his father were getting up to leave when Frank Harris leaped from his seat. "I hope you're happy, punk!" he cried. "I offered you a football career on a platter. You could have been talking to the NFL five years from now. Instead, you'll be working some go-nowhere job. You're washed up. No college team is going to want you now."

Kadeem's father faced Frank Harris.

"Any team will want a young man with his throwing arm and speed!" he shouted. "You're just angry because the kid is on the side of fair play. He holds that as a higher value than playing on a winning team full of illegally recruited players."

Frank Harris waved away Kadeem's father's words. "Ah, you don't know what you're talking about. You'll see."

When Kadeem and his father turned to leave, Kadeem saw that the Channel 39 cameraman was recording it all.

CHAPTER 15

That night, Kadeem sat with his parents in the living room to watch the local news. The first clip they saw was a press conference given by Frank Harris to announce his resignation as assistant coach at Teller. He claimed he had been offered a better position as head coach at a different college. He failed to say what college. Kadeem was pretty sure Frank Harris had simply made it all up to cover the truth. When he was done talking, security guards flanked him on either side and escorted him out of the building.

Hank Rosen came on the screen next. "Citing a long history of recruiting infractions, the NCAA has imposed sanctions on the Teller football team for their failure to abide by the recruitment laws. They will have to give up all their wins for the season. In addition, they will have fewer recruiting days and may employ fewer recruiters. And, most damaging of all, should they become eligible for the championship games this year, they will not be permitted to play."

"Wow!" Kadeem exclaimed. "They really came down hard on them."

"Thanks to you, it looks like they were finally able to catch them at something they've been doing for a long time," his father commented.

"Yeah, thanks to me," Kadeem muttered darkly.

"Don't feel that way," his mother said, patting his shoulder. "I'm proud of what you did." The image on the TV screen caught her eye and she pointed to it excitedly. "Look! It's you and Dad!"

"The NCAA hearing became heated today when Teller's Frank Harris confronted the father of Kadeem Jones. Kadeem is the star quarterback from Southside High who aided the NCAA its investigation of Teller," Hank Rosen reported.

The film that followed showed Mr. Jones telling Frank Harris that Kadeem valued fairness over winning. "Kadeem Jones is an honorable young man we should all feel proud of," Hank Rosen concluded.

"You can say that again!" Mrs. Jones cheered.

"Thanks, Mom," Kadeem said, kissing her cheek as he got off the couch. His cell phone rang and he saw that it was Ty. "I'll take this in my room," he told his parents as he walked out and headed for his bedroom.

"Just saw you on TV," Ty said. "Man, you really blew it for the rest of us."

"Thanks for your support," Kadeem replied dryly.

"What's wrong with some freebies and girls while we're on our way to a huge scholarship? Now there's no Teller for any of us. Thanks loads."

"Where have you been?" Kadeem asked Ty, eager to change the subject. "I haven't seen you in days, not since the game with Uniondale. You never showed to the party."

"I got into a little trouble," Ty said.

"What kind of trouble?"

"On our way to the party, Paige and I sort of got into a fight. I was so upset about blowing the game that I took it out on her."

"What did you do?"

"I kinda hit her—more than once," Ty admitted.

Kadeem was stunned. Ty was wrapped tight, but Kadeem would never have guessed that he'd do something like that.

"Her mother is pressing charges," Ty revealed.

"I don't blame her," Kadeem said. "How could you do something like that?"

"I don't know. I just lost it."

Kadeem shook his head wearily. He felt deeply disappointed in his friend and teammate. Ty was yet another in a growing list of disappointing people Kadeem seemed to be meeting lately. "Catch you later," Kadeem told Ty, hoping later would be a good long while away. He wasn't sure when he'd be in the mood to see Ty again after hearing this latest news.

Kadeem was lying on his bed, staring at the ceiling, when his phone rang again. This number he didn't recognize, but he answered the call anyway. "Don't hang up," said the voice on the other end. He recognized it immediately. "It's me, Alyssa. I'm calling to apologize."

"I'm listening," Kadeem said coldly.

"I know I hurt your feelings, but I thought I was doing the right thing by my team—and by you, too."

"Oh, yeah, sure. I love when girls pretend to like me even though they're just faking. Thanks a lot."

"Well, Teller is a great school with an awesome football team. I didn't think I was hurting you by persuading you to go to school there next year," Alyssa said defensively.

"And did you plan on going out with me once I got there? I don't think so. How was I supposed to feel then?"

"Sorry about that," Alyssa said.

"Not as sorry as I am. Bye." Kadeem shook his head sadly—yet another disappointing person to add to his list.

CHAPTER 16

When he returned to school, Kadeem discovered that his appearance on the nightly news had made him the center of attention. All eyes turned toward him as he walked down the hallway, but he wasn't sure if he was receiving looks of approval or of disgust. Did they think he was a rat who had ruined his teammates' chances at Teller?

The first to come to his locker was Norval Lamb. Kadeem tensed when he saw him approach. "Way to go," Norval said. "I had no idea all that stuff wasn't allowed."

"Me, neither," Kadeem replied. "You aren't mad at me?"

"No way. I don't want to be on a team that gets its players by cheating. Who knows what other crap they're up to? You did the right thing. I don't want to be bought. That's what Teller was doing, if you think about it."

"Thanks, man," Kadeem said. He was impressed that this seemed so clear to Norval, especially since he had had such a tough time deciding what to do. "Does Arnie feel the same way?"

Norval grimaced. "Not exactly. He was hoping for the free ride no matter how he got it."

"Thanks for the heads-up. I'll steer clear," Kadeem said.

"Don't worry. He'll get it eventually. You did right." Norval smiled.

"Thanks," Kadeem said.

"I bet you have a bunch of other offers to fall back on, don't you?" Norval said.

Kadeem shook his head. "Nothing else yet." He wondered how the other recruiters would feel about him. Would they avoid him now?

By seventh period, Kadeem was done with his classes and, as a senior, was allowed to leave early. He was headed for the front door when Coach Green approached him. "Can I talk with you a moment, Kadeem?"

"Sure. What's up?"

"Come to my office," he said, beckoning for Kadeem to follow him back down the hall toward the PE department. When they got there, Kadeem was surprised to see Alan Murphy and Roy Fellows waiting.

They greeted Kadeem warmly. "On behalf of the NCAA, I'd like to present you with a special scholarship for demonstrating outstanding sports ethics," Alan Murphy said. "It's in the amount of fifteen thousand dollars a year, providing you maintain a B average."

"Thank you so much!" Kadeem said, stunned but happy.

Roy Fellows raised a large white envelope. "And here is a solid offer from Peterson, in writing. When you add it to the NCAA scholarship, it should even cover your book bill. We'd love to have you play for Peterson, Kadeem."

Kadeem took the envelope from him. Peterson wasn't the dream team that Teller was, but they were a good, solid team with lots of potential. And if he really thought about it . . . academically, Peterson was stronger than Teller.

"We checked your senior-year grades, and they're on a steady curve upward," Roy Fellows said. "We checked with our admissions department before making this offer. They believe that you're the kind of student they would consider even if you weren't an athlete. Our guys graduate with degrees they've really earned," Roy Fellows added. "You can be truly proud of the degree that you'll get from Peterson."

"I'll keep my grades up," Kadeem assured them.

Coach Green put his hand on Kadeem's shoulder. "See? It pays to do the right thing."

"It does," Kadeem agreed, smiling. "It really does."

CHAPTER 17

Kadeem blasted across the end zone and between the goal posts, holding the football high in triumph! It was the last game of the football season, because they had not made the play-offs. But he had just scored the winning touchdown with a quarterback sneak!

In the stands, the Southside fans roared their approval. What a great way to end the season—with a win! In the next moment, Kadeem was scooped up onto the shoulders of his teammates and carried along. In the stands, he saw his mother and father waving and cheering.

The players deposited him on the sidelines, where Hank Rosen and his cameraman awaited him. "Kadeem, I'd like to follow up on my last story with an interview, if it's all right with you."

This time Kadeem wasn't frozen with fear. "Sure," he agreed, all smiles. "What can I tell you?"

"How are you feeling right now?" Hank Rosen said, with his microphone ready.

"Like a million bucks," Kadeem replied. "Winning always feels great."

"We hear you'll be playing for Peterson next year," Hank Rosen said.

"That's true," Kadeem confirmed.

"We were all amazed how they came from behind to win their conference championship this year," continued the reporter. "Of course, it helped that Teller was out of the competition, but many think that Peterson is the college team to watch."

"Absolutely. They're going to keep getting better and better, too—not to be boastful or anything," Kadeem said with a wink.

"If you play for Peterson like you played today, I'm sure that's true," Hank Rosen agreed. "If things go well at college, are you looking to play pro ball?"

"Count on it," Kadeem confirmed.

About the Author

Suzanne Weyn has written many books for children and young adults. She holds a Masters in Teaching Adolescents and has taught at New York University and City College of New York.

SOUTHSIDE HIGH

ARE YOU A SURVIVOR?

Check out all the books in the

SURVIVING SOUTH SIDE

collection.

Bad Deal

Fish hates having to take ADHD meds. They help him concentrate but also make him feel weird. So when a cute girl needs a boost to study for tests, Fish offers her one of his pills. Soon more kids want pills, and Fish likes the profits. To keep from running out, Fish finds a doctor who sells phony prescriptions. But suddenly the doctor is arrested. Fish realizes he needs to tell the truth. But will that cost him his friends?

Recruited

Kadeem is a star quarterback for Southside High. He is thrilled when college scouts seek him out. One recruiter even introduces him to a college cheerleader and gives him money to have a good time. But then officials start to investigate illegal recruiting. Will Kadeem decide to help their investigation, even though it means the end of the good times? What will it do to his chances of playing in college?

Benito Runs

Benito's father had been in Iraq for over a year. When he returns, Benito's family life is not the same. Dad suffers from PTSD—post-traumatic stress disorder—and yells constantly. Benito can't handle seeing his dad so crazy, so he decides to run away. Will Benny find a new life? Or will he learn how to deal with his dad—through good times and bad?

Plan B

Lucy has her life planned: she'll graduate and join her boyfriend at college in Austin. She'll become a Spanish teacher and of course they'll get married. So there's no reason to wait, right? They try to be careful, but Lucy gets pregnant. Lucy's plan is gone. How will she make the most difficult decision of her life?

Beaten

Keah's a cheerleader and Ty's a football star, so they seem like the perfect couple. But when they have their first fight, Ty is beginning to scare Keah with his anger. Then after losing a game, Ty goes ballistic and hits Keah repeatedly. Ty is arrested for assault, but Keah still secretly meets up with Ty. How can Keah be with someone she's afraid of? What's worse—flinching every time your boyfriend gets angry, or being alone?

Shattered Star

Cassie is the best singer at Southside and dreams of being famous. She skips school to try out for a national talent competition. But her hopes sink when she sees the line. Then a talent agent shows up, and Cassie is flattered to hear she has "the look" he wants. Soon she is lying and missing rehearsal to meet with him. And he's asking her for more each time. How far will Cassie go for her shot at fame?

THE PROTECTORS

Luke's life has never been "normal." How could it be, with
his mother holding séances and his stepfather working as a
mortician? But living in a funeral home never bothered Luke
until the night of his mom's accident.

Sounds of screaming now shatter Luke's dreams. And his
stepfather is acting even stranger. When bodies in the funeral
home start delivering messages, Luke is certain that he's nuts. As
he tries to solve his mother's death, Luke discovers a secret more
horrifying than any nightmare.

SKIN

It looks like a pizza exploded on Nick Barry's face. But bad skin
is the least of his problems. His bones feel like living ice. A
strange rash—like scratches—seems to be some sort of ancient
code. And then there's the anger . . .

Something evil is living under Nick's skin. Where did it
come from? What does it want? With the help of a dead kid's
diary, a nun, and a local professor, Nick slowly finds out what's
wrong with him. But there's still one question that Nick must
face alone: how do you destroy an evil that's *inside* you?

THAW

A July storm caused a major power outage in Bridgewater. Now a research project at the Institute for Cryogenic Experimentation has been ruined, and the thawed-out bodies of twenty-seven federal inmates are missing.

At first, Dani didn't think much of the news. But after her best friend Jake disappears, a mysterious visitor connects the dots for Dani. Jake has been taken in by a cult. To get him back, Dani must enter a dangerous, alternate reality where a defrosted cult leader is beginning to act like some kind of god.

UNTHINKABLE

Omar Phillips is Bridgewater High's favorite teen author. His fans can't wait for his next horror story. But lately Omar's imagination has turned against him. Horrifying visions of death and destruction haunt him. The only way to stop the visions is to write them down. Until they start coming true . . .

Enter Sophie Minax, the mysterious girl who's been following Omar at school. "I'm one of you," Sophie says. She tells Omar how to end the visions—but the only thing worse than Sophie's cure may be what happens if he ignores it.

THE CLUB

The club started innocently enough. Bored after school, Josh and his friends decided to try out an old board game. Called "Black Magic," it promised players good fortune at the expense of those who have wronged them.

But when the club members' luck starts skyrocketing—and horror befalls their enemies—the game stops being a joke. How can they stop what they've unleashed? Answers lie in an old diary—but ending the game may be deadlier than any curse.

MESSAGES FROM BEYOND

Some guy named Ethan has been texting Cassie. He seems to know all about her—but she can't place him. He's not in the yearbook either. Cassie thinks one of her friends is punking her. But she can't ignore the strange coincidences—like how Ethan looks just like the guy in her nightmares.

Cassie's search for Ethan leads her to a shocking discovery—and a struggle for her life. Will Cassie be able to break free from her mysterious stalker?